This book belongs to...

_____

© Illus. Dr. Seuss 1957

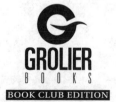

GROLIER
B O O K S

BOOK CLUB EDITION

Pizza Pat

A pizza toast for a real hero:
To Felip Restrepo with love.
—r. g. g.

Text copyright © 1999 by Rita Gelman. Illustrations copyright © 1999 by Will Terry.
All rights reserved under International and Pan-American Copyright Conventions.
Published in the United States by Random House, Inc., New York, and simultaneously
in Canada by Random House of Canada Limited, Toronto.

www.randomhouse.com/kids

Library of Congress Cataloging-in-Publication Data
Gelman, Rita Golden.
Pizza Pat / by Rita Gelman ; illustrated by Will Terry.   p.   cm. — (Step into reading.
A step 1 book)   Summary: A cumulative rhyme describes the choppy cheese, sloppy
sausages, gloppy tomatoes, and floppy dough that are cooked into a pizza and
enjoyed by dozens of mice.   ISBN 0-679-89134-X (pbk.) — ISBN 0-679-99134-4
(lib. bdg.)   [1. Pizza—Fiction. 2. Mice—Fiction. 3. Stories in rhyme.]
I. Terry, Will, 1956– ill. II. Title. III. Series: Step into reading. Step 1 book.
PZ8.3.G28Pi   1999   [E]—dc21   97-44609

Printed in the United States of America 10 9 8 7 6 5 4 3 2 1

BRIGHT & EARLY BOOKS is a registered trademark of Random House, Inc.

Pizza Pat

by Rita Golden Gelman
illustrated by Will Terry

A Bright & Early Book
From BEGINNER BOOKS
A Division of Random House, Inc.

Random House 🏠 New York

This is Pat.

This is the tray

that Pat bought.

This is the dough,
all stretchy and floppy,

that lay in the tray

that Pat bought.

This is the sauce,
all gooey and gloppy,

that covered the dough,
all stretchy and floppy,
that lay in the tray
that Pat bought.

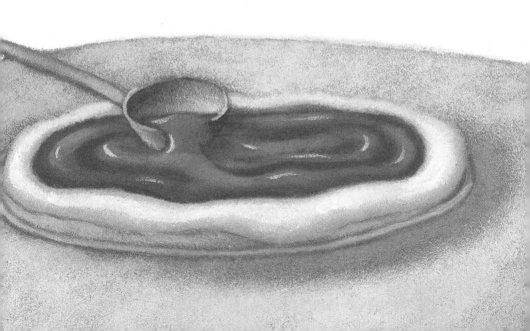

These are the sausages,

spicy and choppy,

that sat on the sauce,

all gooey and gloppy,

that covered the dough,

all stretchy and floppy,

that lay in the tray

that Pat bought.

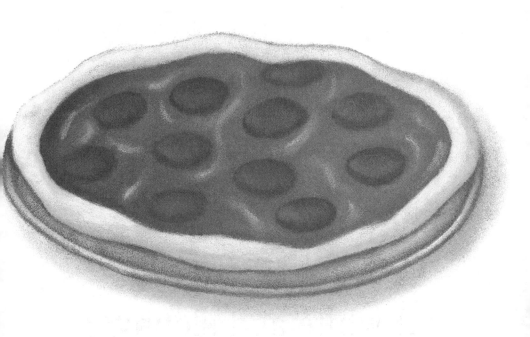

This is the cheese,
all white and sloppy,

that topped the sausages,
spicy and choppy,

that sat on the sauce,
all gooey and gloppy,
that covered the dough,
all stretchy and floppy,
that lay in the tray
that Pat bought.

This is the oven,

800 degrees,

that cooked the pizza

and melted the cheese

that topped the sausages,

spicy and choppy,

that sat on the sauce,

all gooey and gloppy,

that covered the dough,
all stretchy and floppy,
that lay in the tray
that Pat bought.

This is the pizza,
all cooked and chewy
and spicy and sloppy
and gloppy and gooey.

These are the mice,
their friends,
and their cousins.
Mice from the
neighborhood.
Mice by the dozens!

They stole the pizza,
all cooked and chewy
and spicy and sloppy
and gloppy and gooey.

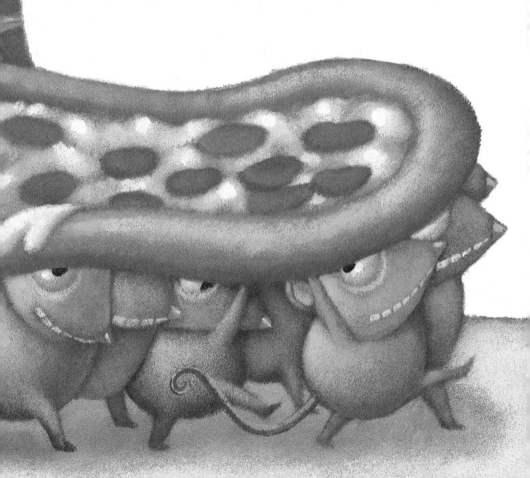

It came from the oven,
800 degrees,
that cooked the pizza
and melted the cheese
that topped the sausages,
spicy and choppy,

that sat on the sauce,

all gooey and gloppy,

that covered the dough,

all stretchy and floppy,

that lay in the tray

that Pat bought.

This is the tray
that Pat bought.

This is Pat.

Poor Pat.